THE CAT WHO ATE CHRISTMAS

With thanks to Freya

LITTLE, BROWN BOOKS FOR YOUNG READERS

First published in Great Britain in 2016 by Hodder and Stoughton

1 3 5 7 9 10 8 6 4 2

A CIP catalogue record for this book
is available from the British Library.

ISBN 978-1-51020-082-1

Printed and bound in Italy

The paper and board used in this book are
made from wood from responsible sources.

Little, Brown Books for Young Readers
An imprint of
Hachette Children's Group
Part of Hodder and Stoughton
Carmelite House
50 Victoria Embankment
London EC4Y 0DZ

An Hachette UK Company
www.hachette.co.uk

www.hachettechildrens.co.uk

THE CAT WHO ATE CHRISTMAS

LIL CHASE & THOMAS DOCHERTY

LITTLE, BROWN BOOKS FOR YOUNG READERS
www.lbkids.co.uk

It was Christmas Eve.

"Here, Jingles! Look nice for Santa." Rose reached for the kitten and tried to tie a piece of tinsel to his tail.

"*Yowl!*" Jingles didn't like anyone touching his tail.

He sprang from the chair . . . on to the mantelpiece . . . and straight on to the Christmas tree.

"*Miaow!*"

The tree tilted, and the angel toppled. Jingles leapt to the floor, his paws skidding on a piece of wrapping paper.

"Oh, Jingles!" cried Lily as she caught the angel.

Jingles raced out of the room. Alex tried
to catch him but his arms closed around
thin air. "Did you know that there are six
hundred million cats in the world?" he
said. "But only one as naughty as Jingles!"

"Quick! Before Mum and Dad see."
Lily *heeeeeaved* the tree upright. *Oof!*
They hung up the decorations again.

"Mum spent ages making these,"
said Alex, as he smoothed out the bent
corners of a tinfoil star.

Lily straightened the angel's dress.
"Now they're as good as new."

"Time to hang up your stockings!" Dad called from the kitchen.

"Should we leave a treat for the reindeers?" asked Lily.

"Reindeers like carrots," Alex told them.

"Jingles needs a treat," said Rose.

"Now, into your PJs. Quick!" said Mum, as she chased them upstairs.

Pyjamas on.

Teeth done.

Teeth inspected.

Teeth done again.

Into bed!

15

"I hope Father Christmas brings me new ballet shoes," said Lily.

"I want a book of fascinating facts!" said Alex.

"I want to cuddle Jingles," said Rose.

"Did you know," yawned Alex, "that the tallest Christmas tree was over sixty-seven metres tall?"

Dad ruffled Alex's hair. "Did *you* know that if you're not asleep when Father Christmas arrives he won't leave you anything?"

Alex squeezed his eyes tight shut.

"If you see Father Christmas," said Mum, as she turned out the light, "please say 'Merry Christmas' from me."

Then Alex, Lily and Rose were each given ...

a kiss

and a hug

and a look that said,
Go to sleep now.

Mum scooped up Jingles and left the bedroom, pulling the door almost shut.

"Good night," Rose murmured.
"Good …" Lily began to say, but
the rest of her words fell away.

If Lily had still been
awake, she would have
seen ...

... that a visitor had
arrived!

The next morning, the children ran into their parents' room.

"It's **CHRISTMAS DAY!**"

"Time to get up!"

Dad rubbed his eyes. "It's five-thirty in the morning," he said, yawning.

"It's ten-thirty in India," Alex said. "Come on!"

One step, two steps, three steps ...
They crept down the stairs.

Then Lily snapped on a light and ...

They froze.

"What … ?" asked Lily.

"When … ?" whispered Alex.

"How … ?" said Dad, peering over the tops of their heads.

Jingles leapt from Rose's arms.

"All your lovely decorations," said Lily, putting her hand in Mum's hand.

The family followed Jingles into the living room.

"The presents are all unwrapped!" said Alex, stepping over a pile of crumpled wrapping paper.

"*Miaow!*"

Jingles was at the top of the Christmas tree. He didn't look happy at all.

Rose heaved a big breath.
Dad tried to get to her but—

**"WAHHHHHHHH!
JINGLES BROKE
CHRISTMAS."**

Jingles winced. His fur stood up on end and then …

Creeeeeeak.

CRASH!

The tree collapsed into a heap of glitter and tinsel.

"Oh, Jingles!" cried Mum.

How had one little kitten done all this?

"What a naughty cat," Dad said to Mum, looking at the decorations Mum had spent so long making.

"Naughty cat!" said Rose.

"I can fix them," said Mum. "You go and find Jingles. Tell him I'm not cross," she added. "Not really."

Jingles was hiding under the bed.

The children waved Jingles' favourite things at him.

"Here, little kitten," said Alex.

"We're not cross," said Lily. "Not really."

But Jingles didn't want to come out.

"Jingles will appear when he's ready," said Mum.

"Cocoa," said Dad. "The fix for everything. Even a broken Christmas."

After breakfast, Lily, Alex and Rose played with their presents. Everyone forgot how naughty Jingles had been.

Mum whistled as she took the turkey out of the oven. Dad hummed as he set the table.

"There. Christmas is perfect again," said Dad.

"Let's go and get Grandma," said Mum.

"Yay!" The children jumped up.

Mum bundled Rose into a scarf while
Lily pulled on her new bobble hat and Alex
climbed into his wellington boots.

"Where's Jingles?" asked Dad. "We don't want him ruining your decorations again, love."

"Naughty cat!" said Rose.

"I'll make sure he's upstairs," said Lily.

Jingles was still hiding.

"We're going to get Grandma, Jingles," Lily told him. "We'll be back in time for lunch."

"Come on, Lily!" called Dad's voice.

"You stay here, out of trouble," she told
Jingles. Then she leapt to her feet and
ran downstairs, quickly shutting the door
behind her.

Too quickly …

CREEEEEEAK ...

SNIFF ...

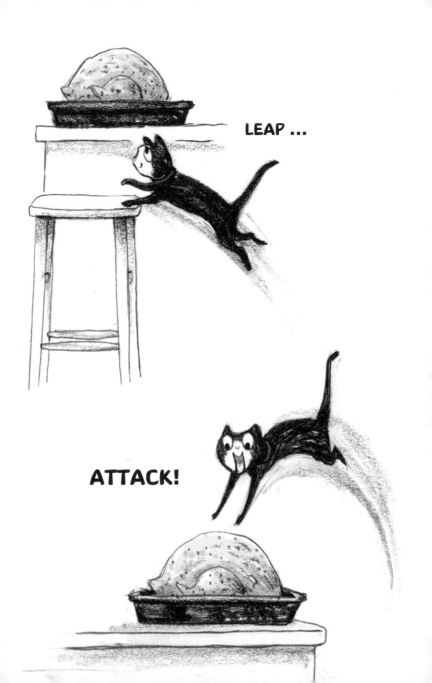

It didn't take long to get to Grandma's house, even through the snow.

The children couldn't wait to tell her all about their presents.

"How's Jingles?" Grandma asked Mum.

"He's under the bed," said Alex. "In disgrace."

"He ruined Mum's decorations," Lily explained.

"He's a naughty cat," added Rose.

"He's … Jingles," Mum replied with a sigh.

Everyone was really hungry when they got back from Grandma's.

"I can't wait to eat Mum's special Christmas turkey," said Dad.

"*Deeelicious*," said Rose.

Dad opened the back door, stepped into the kitchen and …

… slid across the kitchen floor.

"ARGHHHH!"

"What … ?" asked Grandma.

"When … ?" whispered Alex.

"How … ?" wondered Lily.

"Jingles!" said Mum. "You ate my TURKEY!"

Rose's bottom lip quivered.

"WAHHHHHHHHHH! JINGLES ATE CHRISTMAS!"

"Jingles was very hungry," said Lily,
throwing chewed parsnips into the bin.

"Jingles was very lucky," said Grandma, picking up what was left of the turkey.

"Jingles was very naughty," said Rose.

"Where *is* Jingles?" asked Alex.

They all went outside to look for their naughty kitten.

"I think he ran away because we shouted," said Lily, in a worried voice.

"I wasn't really cross with Jingles," said Mum. "Not *really*."

"I want Jingles!" said Rose.

"We'll find him," said Dad. "Come on."

They went and asked the neighbours. No Jingles.

They kept looking,

and walking,

and looking,

all the way into town.

No Jingles.

"Jingles doesn't like singing,"
said Alex. "He especially
doesn't like Rose's singing."

Lily twisted her plaits. She
did that when she was worried.

They went to the park.

No Jingles.

"This is no good!" cried Lily, chewing her plaits.

Jingles was happiest when he was at home. That was where he should be.

"Maybe he'll come home all by himself," said Mum.

"Come on," said Grandma. "It's getting dark. Let's head back. You can drop me off on the way."

But when they got home, the house was empty.

"Jingles has never stayed away from home before," said Alex.

"He'll be all right," said Dad.

"I wonder what he's doing?" said Lily.

"I'm sure he's having fun!" said their mum.

That night, everyone dreamed of Jingles.

The next morning, Lily and Alex didn't want any breakfast.

"Jingles loves breakfast," said Lily.

"We should fill his bowl as usual," said Alex. "Then maybe he'll come home."

Rose stood on her tiptoes and opened the cupboard.

"No cat food!" she cried.

Alex, Lily and Rose ran to Mum and
Dad. "Come on! Come on! We need to go
to the supermarket. RIGHT NOW!"
There wasn't even time to get dressed.

When they got to the supermarket,
Grandma was arriving to start work.

"What a nice surprise!" Grandma said,
hugging them. "What are you doing here?"

"We've run out of food for Jingles," said Alex.

"We need to buy more so he'll come home," said Lily.

It took a long time to get to the pet food aisle. Everyone kept stopping to say "Happy Christmas!"

Jingles' favourite turkey treats were on the top shelf.

Alex, Lily and Rose reached up to get them.

Mum and Dad came to help.

"What else would Jingles like?" asked Mum.

Lily chose a bright red collar.

Alex picked a scratching post.

Rose wanted a toy mouse.

"He'll definitely come home when he hears this!" Lily shook the packet of treats.

They went to the checkout to pay for
everything, daydreaming about their kitten
coming home.

Beep! Beep! Beep! Beep! "**MIAOW!**"

"Jingles! You came back!"

"A cat?!" said the man behind the till.

"Our kitten ran away," Alex explained.

"Naughty cat," said Rose.

"Where have you been?" Lily asked.

Grandma suddenly guessed where Jingles had been hiding. (Can you?)

Mum paid. Dad packed the bags.

It was time to take Jingles home.

Back at home, they played with
Jingles and his new toys until it
was time for bed.

Pyjamas on.

Teeth done.

Teeth inspected.

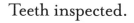

Perfect!

Jingles made himself comfy on Lily's pillow. She sighed and smiled and gazed up at the skylight.

"Did you see … ?" asked Alex.

"I did!" said Lily.

"Father Christmas!" gasped Rose.

"Maybe he didn't want to leave until he knew Jingles was safe," wondered Lily.

"Until he knew we had everything we wanted for Christmas," Alex said.

"Go to sleep now," said Mum, with her serious look. But she wasn't cross, not really.

"Jingles ate Christmas," said Rose. Everyone laughed.

"He did," said Mum. "But we'll always love him."

As the bedroom door closed, Lily's eyelids grew heavy. It had been a long day.

"Good night," murmured Alex.

"Night, night," said Rose.

"We love you, Jingles," said Lily, reaching out to stroke their cat. Her hand closed around thin air. Her eyes snapped open. "Where's ..."

ALEX'S CHRISTMAS FACTS

Alex loves facts. Here are some of his favourite facts about Christmas — and cats!

The tallest ever Christmas tree was displayed in 1950 at the Northgate Shopping Center in Seattle, Washington. It was 67.36 metres tall!

Cats can hear better than dogs — and humans!

Santa has nine reindeer. Their names are Dasher, Dancer, Prancer, Vixen, Comet, Cupid, Donner and Blitzen — and of course Rudolph, who leads the way with his glowing red nose.

Where do you leave your stocking for Santa? In some countries, children don't have a Christmas stocking! In France, Germany, Mexico and Iceland, children put their shoes by the window or under the Christmas tree to be filled with presents.

In North and North-West India, Christmas Day is known as 'Badaa Din' which means 'Big Day'.

Cats love to sleep. In fact, they spend about two-thirds of their whole lives sleeping! Zzzzz ...

Has your cat ever
eaten your turkey?
Never mind. If you lived in
Poland or Slovakia, you'd be eating
a fish called carp for Christmas dinner!

The world record for the
fastest time to decorate a Christmas tree is
held by Sharon Juantuah from Essex. She
decorated her tree in just 36.89 seconds!

A male cat is called a tom, and a
female cat is called a
queen or a molly.

CHRISTMAS CRACKER JOKES

Q. What do you get if you cross Santa with a duck?
A. A Christmas quacker!

Q. What is Father Christmas's dog called?
A. Santa Paws!

Q. What do you get if you cross a Christmas bell with a skunk?
A. Jingle Smells!

Oh, oh, oh !

Q. What goes 'Oh oh oh'?
A. Santa walking backwards!

Q. Why did the turkey cross the road?
A. Because it was the chicken's day off!

Q. Who hides in the bakery at Christmas?
A. Mince spies!

Q. What did one snowman say to the other snowman?
A. I can smell carrots!

HOW TO MAKE COCOA

Dad made cocoa to cheer everyone up after Jingles caused chaos! Here's the recipe so you can enjoy it too. You will need a grown-up to help you.

INGREDIENTS:

1 pint of milk

1 tablespoon of icing sugar

2 tablespoons of cocoa powder

50g dark chocolate, finely grated (ask a grown-up to do this for you!)

½ teaspoon ground cinnamon (optional)

Whipped cream, marshmallows, sprinkles (optional, for decorating)

METHOD:

1. Pour the milk into a large saucepan. Ask a grown-up to turn the heat up to medium, and wait until it is simmering gently (not boiling).

2. Add the icing sugar, cocoa powder, grated chocolate and cinnamon. With the pan still on the heat, whisk for a couple of minutes until all the ingredients are mixed.

3. Ask a grown-up to carefully pour the hot cocoa into mugs. Add whipped cream, marshmallows and sprinkles to decorate, if you want.

4. Drink your cocoa and try not to get a chocolate moustache!

HOW TO MAKE A
CHRISTMAS ANGEL

In the story, Mum is an artist and has made lots of the beautiful Christmas decorations. Here's how you can make your own Christmas angel to go on top of your tree.

You will need:

- A toilet roll tube

- Stiff card (for the angel's wings — any colour you like)

- Wool, string or strips of fabric or paper (for the angel's hair — any colour you like)

- Coloured pens, pencils or paint

- Child-friendly scissors

- A glue stick

- Any decorations that you like! You could use sequins, stickers, tinsel, feathers, shapes cut out of coloured paper or fabric, etc.

- Our template for the angel's wings (p.95). You can trace it or ask a grown-up to photocopy it for you.

METHOD:

1. Use the template on the next page to draw the outline of the angel's wings on your stiff card. Cut out and decorate as you like. If you have feathers, you could glue them on!

2. Glue the wings on to the back of the toilet roll tube as in the picture here.

3. Glue the angel's hair on to the top of the tube as in the picture below. Leave room for her face!

4. Draw the angel's face. You can also decorate the rest of the tube with your coloured pens, pencils or paint, and any decorations you have.

5. When the glue is dry, you can ask a grown-up to put your angel on top of the Christmas tree.

ABOUT THE AUTHOR

Lil Chase lives in London with her husband and daughter. Having been a pub cook and even suffered a brief stint in Disneyland Paris, she settled on a career in her first love – telling stories. Visit her online at www.lilchase.com.

ABOUT THE ILLUSTRATOR

Thomas Docherty is an acclaimed author and illustrator of children's picture books including *Little Boat*, *Big Scary Monster*, *The Driftwood Ball* and Jenny Colgan's *Polly and the Puffin* series. *The Snatchabook*, which was written by his wife Helen, has been shortlisted for several awards in the UK and US and has been translated into 17 languages.

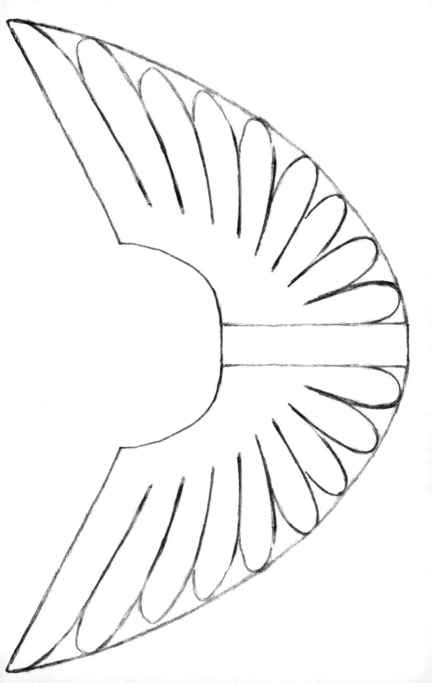

CONGRATULATIONS!

Congratulations to Millie from
Fairways Primary School, who won
the competition to name the kitten
in this book with her suggestion of
"Jingles". A big thank you to Millie,
and to all the children who entered
the competition, which was hosted by
Lovereading4kids.co.uk.